THE AMBER DAME

BOOKS BY BRENDAN NOBLE

The Realm Reachers:
The Crimson Court

Realm Reacher Novellas:
The Amber Dame

The Frostmarked Chronicles:
A Dagger in the Winds
The Trials of Ascension
The Daughters of the Earth
The Deathless Sons

Frostmarked Tales:
The Rider in the Night
The Lady of Rolika

The Prism Files:
The Fractured Prism
Crimson Reigns
Pridefall
White Crown

Author Note: Trigger Warning

The Amber Dame contains elements that may be triggers or traumatic to some readers, so please proceed with caution if any of the below are so for you. I have done my best to treat these serious topics carefully and with respect.

- Mental illness
- Death
- Torture
- Graphic injury

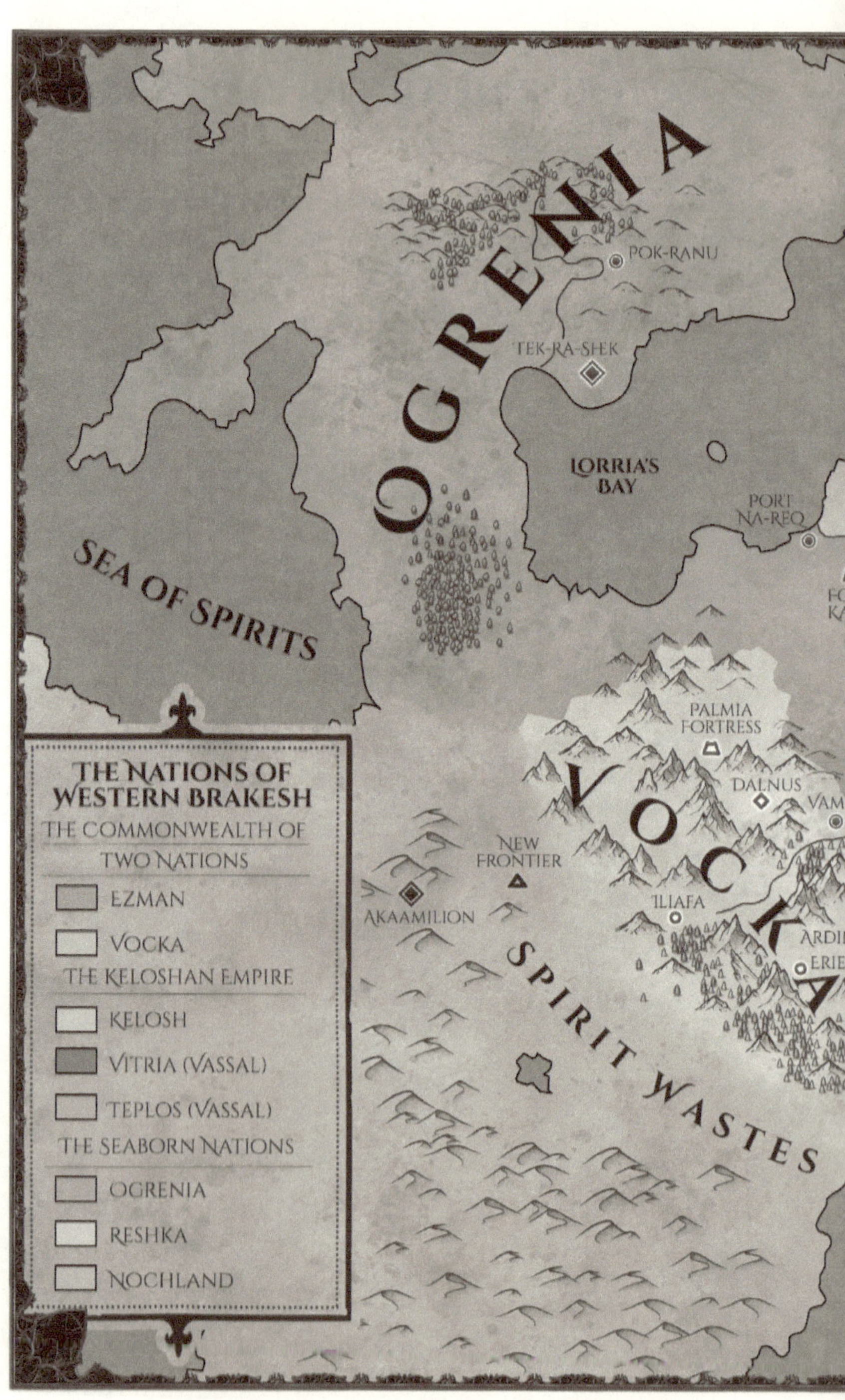
OGRENIA
POK-RANU
TEK-RA-SIEK
LORRIA'S BAY
PORT NA-REQ
SEA OF SPIRITS
PALMIA FORTRESS
DALNUS
VAM
VOCKA
NEW FRONTIER
ARDIN
ERIE
AKAAMILION
ILIAFA
FO
KA
SPIRIT WASTES
THE NATIONS OF WESTERN BRAKESH
THE COMMONWEALTH OF TWO NATIONS
EZMAN
VOCKA
THE KELOSHAN EMPIRE
KELOSH
VITRIA (VASSAL)
TEPLOS (VASSAL)
THE SEABORN NATIONS
OGRENIA
RESHKA
NOCHLAND

VITRIAN SEA
VITRIA
KELOSH
ORIOKSTAK
ISLE OF BALAN
LITIANITAN
NOCHLAND
ALA RIVER
ZAKINIV
KALASTOK
ANUKIT
LOST BROTHERS' FORTS
ZMAN
TEPLOS
REXANIV
RAVIAK FOREST
GIAMIVIK
TYSTOK
JAANIIK
UVANESS
NIMASTOK
RESHKAN COLONIES
GULF OF NIMAZ
NIIMAA FORTRESS
LOONAANII CHANNEL
RESHKA
ESHKANAA

GLASSBLADE
ORDER
HOUSE
PIKEZIK
KAL
COMMONWEALTH
SPHERES OF
INFLUENCE
EZMANI GREAT HOUSES
HOUSE BARTOL
HOUSE KUZON
HOUSE OLIEZANY
HOUSE PIKEZIK
HOUSE UZIOKAKI
VOCKAN GREAT HOUSES
AND ORDERS
HOUSE IZ ARDINVIL
GLASSBLADE ORDER
FALLEN HOUSES
HOUSE NIEZIK
HOUSE
IZ ARDINVIL

HOUSE
CZANY
TOK
HOUSE
BARTOI
HOUSE
UZIOKAKI
HOUSE
NIEZIK
HOUSE
KUZON

THE KNOWN REALMS

Realm	Reacher Power	Color
Air	Summon and control air/wind	Sky Blue
Body	Heal and strengthen bodies	Blood Red
Dark	Summon complete darkness and see within it	Black
Death	Kill target's body and spirit	Purple
Earth	Manipulate earth, alter metals, call earthquakes	Brown
Fire	Summon and control fire	Orange
Force	Call force fields and blasts of energy (or smaller pushes)	Bright Red
Life	Create plants and encourage their growth/Grant life energy to a target who is near death	Green
Light	Summon pure light and see no matter how bright	Yellow
Mind	Manipulate a target's thoughts	Pink
Possibility	Alter odds/Summon objects	Rainbow
Shadow	Summon shadows and see through them	Dark Gray
Spirit	Repel spirits or guide them into newborns	Silver
Truth	Compel target to speak the truth or halt/Mend broken objects (inorganic)	White
Water	Summon and control water	Navy Blue

House Emblems

NIEZIK*

UZIOKAKI

BARTOL

OLIEZANY

KUZON

PIKEZIK

IZ ARDINVIL

IZ VAMIUSTOK*

*Not Great Houses. Included for reference

THE AMBER DAME

BRENDAN NOBLE

RAVIAK FOREST

The eastern gales swept through Raviak Forest with an unwelcome chill, shivering auburn and scarlet leaves off the trees as Lady Katarzyna Niezik pulled up her coat's fur-lined collar. By the spirits, the duskfall season's chilled rain refused to relent. She had no time for such delays.

"A storm's brewing, my lady," Artaxan said as he slowed his horse. A tall, bulky man dressed in an unbuttoned leather duster and Ogrenian tricorn hat, he resembled a common brawler more than a chief scout. Still, she trusted him. He'd discovered the amber she now sought, after all.

She gritted her teeth and pushed her deep bay horse into a trot. "I do not lack eyes, but if we tarry for every drop of rain, we shall be in these woods until everdark falls. Every day we spend in these motherforsaken woods is another for House Uziokaki to interfere."

Another rider pulled up beside her, resting a hand on her arm. "Perhaps Artaxan is right, Kasia," her footman and loyal friend, Tazper, whispered. He used the informal version of her name, but she preferred it, despising the unneeded *Z* in *Katarzyna* that Ezmani scions loved to include in their children's names. "We have ridden hard for a few days now. I am sure we could all use the rest and shelter."

Kasia tossed away the ashen gray hair—just darker than her pale-gray skin—that had fallen over her shoulder. Did no one else care about House Niezik's survival? Without full access to the disputed forest and its amber, she would be forced to sell what remained of the assets her father, Leonit, and his predecessors had gathered over the centuries. His businesses and foreign artifacts were all she had left of him. She refused to lose them.

"Who else believes it is better to stop?" she shouted over the brewing storm.

They had a dozen riders, and all but her raised their hands. Artaxan sat taller when Kasia looked ahead to him. "Most of us have spent over a dozen seasons in these woods, my lady," he said. "Trust that we know when it is best to take shelter."

"Fine, then." She waved a gloved hand toward the trees. "Let us make camp for the night, but we continue the moment the storm passes."

"You heard Lady Katarzyna!" Artaxan pointed to the other scouts, then to the western edge of a nearby hill. "Ready the tents. We've not got long until we're all soaked to the bone."

The scouts rushed toward the hill with the final horse pulling the supply cart. Kasia cursed her sore bottom as she followed with Tazper. Most of her traveling had been via carriage since a young age, and she'd not ridden this long in her twenty-two years of life. Artaxan had tried to improve her seat during the first days, but her spite had silenced those attempts. She didn't need to be a skilled rider.

She needed amber.

"These men and women are loyal to you," Tazper said he dismounted and helped Kasia do the same.

She took his hand, but her foot twisted in the stirrup. It slipped free at the wrong moment, and she tumbled into Tazper, taking him to the ground. He laughed amid the roots and fallen leaves.

"Well, that is certainly one way to do it."

Kasia shook her head at herself. How did the scouts make it look so easy? "Knights in shining armor are supposed to catch the damsel," she quipped, brushing off her breeches on the ground.

Tazper stood and offered her his hand again. "Then it's all fine and well that I am a footman in a dirtied wool coat. The expectations are *far* more reasonable."

"One must rise to their position," she replied, using his hand as an anchor to stand. The move brought them uncomfortably close, so she stepped away to not draw any curious eyes. Though Tazper was more of a brother to her than her actual brother, Gregorzon, everyone insisted on questioning whether they were mere friends. The last thing she needed was rumors of promiscuity.

She waited at the edge of camp as Tazper left to set up her tent, then his own. Most of the scouts were lowborn, but even noble scions from minor families, like Tazper and the three magic-wielding Realm Reachers they had brought, had to do most of their own labor. Kasia was a matriarch. She couldn't be seen doing a task as menial as tent building. Her father had taught her much, and the greatest lesson of all was that perception drives influence. It mattered not how false a person's perception of her was, as long as it was favorable to her interests.

Two of the other scions, Lazan and Fanzala, worked in sync as Body and Earth Reachers respectively. The crystalline talon-like blades they wore wrapped around their left index fingers allowed them to Reach into their bonded realm and draw magic from it.

Fanzala morphed the hillside into an archway that covered the flimsy tents as Lazan lent the scouts extra strength to work through their exhaustion. Fanzala's creation was beautiful as the low, horizon-level light of the duskfall season split through the archway. But cracks dispersed across it. Kasia hoped they wouldn't damage the structure.

Though inexperienced, the Reachers they had were all she could afford to hire. No amber mine could be built quickly without an Earth Reacher to dig and Body Reacher to aid miners. They would have to be enough.

Except, where was Harizik?

Kasia kept her worries about the arch to herself as she scanned the camp for her Spirit Reacher. Everyone in the group had glass shards in case a rogue awakened spirit attacked—other weapons would do nothing against them—but Harizik would be their only real protection. Had he run off *again*?

"You have one job…" she muttered, stomping up the hill to get a better vantage point.

Along the way, she pondered why she hadn't followed the easy path and become a Spirit Reacher. They were the most prized of any Reacher, bonded to this realm—Zekiaz—and a single one could protect entire villages if they were skilled. Harizik certainly thought he was. The coward had all but run from every harmless drifter spirit they had seen so far, though, and when Kasia spotted a few drifters hanging overhead, she shook her head.

"They are not awakened!" she called into the dim forest. "And even if they were, you're the one who's supposed to stop them."

A stout, square-chinned man wearing an obscenely long black cape stepped out from behind a nearby oak, rubbing his talon like it were some mythical Reshkan lamp. "I was getting a better angle. That's all."

Kasia scoffed as Harizik neared. He had a pinkish undertone to his skin that was rare among Ezmani scions, so she assumed he had lowborn blood in him. That was no excuse for cowardice. She'd seen lowborn far more capable than the influential scions of the great houses, and Harizik was neither capable nor influential.

"If I lose a scout because you are hiding," she snapped, "then I will send pamphlets from Tystok to Vocka proclaiming you are not worth a single kena. You begged me for another chance after the awakened attack in everbright, so prove to me you deserve it."

His head dropped. "Yes, Lady Katarzyna."

She corrected most people to call her Kasia, but that required respect—and respect was *earned*. So, instead, she nodded toward the camp. "Go get some rest. Just because you are a Spirit Reacher who's afraid of spirits, that doesn't mean you deserve to rot in the storm to come."

He trudged away with his hands stuffed in his coat pockets. Kasia's spite lingered in his wake, and she winced at the memories of her last Reach into her own realm: Death.

A Death Reacher who is afraid of death, she thought. *Am I any less pathetic than him?*

Her heart ached as she headed toward Fanzala's arch, overlooking the camp with the face of her former lover, Aliax, burned in her memories. She'd not Reached since that day three years before, and his voice haunted her—the voice of the man she'd killed.

"You'd have loved this trip," she told him. "Forests, duskfall leaves, and plenty of time alone in a tent."

Priestesses of the Crystal Mother claimed mourning faded over time, but Kasia's breaths were shallow even now, as if the void in her chest had consumed her lungs. Grief was its own monster. Guilt, though, was greater. It reminded her with each beat of her heart that she was the reason for her pain, her loneliness. She'd sought this power, not that of any other kind of Reacher, and in turn, the Spirit Crystal had granted her the tool she desired for revenge. Except all it had brought was more loss.

It's better this way, she reminded herself. *My Reaching is dangerous, and so am I.*

A *snap* tore her from her thoughts. She spun toward the sound, pulling her revolver, but she'd barely shot before. Her hands shook as she stared into eyes as black as coals, a beast's sheer black fur merging with the shadows despite towering into the branches above.

A male koilee.

"I am not a threat," she told it, retreating toward Fanzala's arch. The ledge lay just strides behind her, and the faintest whimpering rose from it.

The koilee growled, exposing teeth as long as her forearm, and advanced slowly. Sharp quills jutted from every visible part of the bear-like creature's body, coated in a paralyzing poison that protected even the youngest of their kind. Almost mythical for their ruthlessness, koilee were feared all throughout the Commonwealth of Two Nations. That ruthlessness and their poison made a koilee pelt as valuable as a shipment of amber, but that only mattered if one survived the encounter. A pistol surely wouldn't be enough to down it. Nothing, though, could survive a Death Reacher's blast.

"Death isn't the answer," Aliax said in her head, his death echoing through her life.

Kasia stepped back as she removed the glove over her left hand's Reacher talon, then stopped. No… Aliax was right. Reaching could kill a beast like this, but what if she lost control of her power again? Who else would she lose?

"Face the beast with your wit!" Aliax insisted. *"You're more than a scared animal."*

Another noise came from behind her, and the koilee rose onto its hind legs as the storm struck. Trees trembled as rain swept over the forest with a mighty gust that pushed Kasia to the ledge. There was nowhere to run, and she could hardly negotiate with an enraged animal. So she fired.

The bullet flew wide.

"I promised you, Ali," she whispered, "but you're dead. Let me Reach."

"Am I dead if you can still hear me?"

Kasia hesitated. The koilee didn't.

The arch crumbled underfoot as the beast slammed into her. She fired wildly. Her ears rang, and recoil flung the revolver from her grasp as she tumbled over the edge.

"Tazper!"

Kasia flailed, desperate for *something* to grab hold of. But there was only the stinging rain and a flash of fur out of the corner of her eye. A squeaked cry came from it, lost in the thunder that rolled overhead.

The drop was no more than thirty feet, but it felt as if she fell forever, helplessness consuming her every breath. What was the ability to kill any foe if she could not use it when it mattered most?

No answers came before she struck the ground. It was softer than it should've been, its mud molding around her body as brown wisps of Fanzala's Earth Reaching surrounded her. Pain came regardless.

"Kasia?" Tazper exclaimed, rushing to her with the others. "Kasia, are you okay?"

Kasia's head spun as she looked from him to the blurry remains of the arch. The koilee's front legs hung over the ledge, stretching out for the tuft of fur she'd seen clinging to the edge.

"It's a father," she mumbled.

Shots rang out, followed by a horrible cry, then a higher pitched one. Kasia tried to see what had become of the beast, but Lazan held her down, red wisps circling his taloned hand. He had a gentle face and an even gentler touch. His cold crystal talon against her skin, though, was enough to make her squirm.

"All will be well," Lazan reassured her. "The wounds will heal."

His words were like the drifting vapors of a lost spirit. A final *bang* rose over them, and the massive koilee fell from the cliff, shaking the ground when it landed just strides away. Yet again, Lazan kept her looking up the slope as the scouts carried her off. The smaller koilee struggled at the edge of her vision. Scouts shot at it, but it reached the arch's peak and clambered over the edge.

When the rainfall ceased beneath the cover of the undamaged section of Fanzala's arch, Kasia found her eyes still wet. Not from her injuries, but the pain in her heart.

That cub is an orphan now.

She had come between a father and its child. Fanzala altering the landscape had sent the cub over the ledge, hanging on for dear life, and its father had given everything to protect it. Just as Leonit had done for her ten years before.

Darkness crept through her vision, and in her final waking moments, a wispy visage of her father stood over her. He held a book in one hand and his spectacles in the other. His expression, though, was fuzzy, inconstant. One moment, he gave the closed smile that was his equivalent of beaming, and the next, he glared at her with discontent.

I'll make you proud, Father. I promise.

THE HUNTERS

"I'll not be listening to another word from you Uziokaki scum."

Kasia groaned as she awoke to Artaxan's voice carrying from outside her mid-sized tent. Her tent? She glanced around, the dim light through the canvas barely enough to see that she was on her bedroll. Blankets covered her, but she was *freezing*.

Her cheeks burned as she checked her clothes. The scouts had stripped her of her drenched outer layers, but had left her shift on. It was dry despite the rain that had soaked her coat. Her hair, though, had been exposed, its damp chill now stinging against her skin. She'd not brought her handmaiden, Kikania, out of worry the girl would be ill fit for such a journey. This morning, though, she regretted that choice.

She pried herself free from the embrace of her blankets and dressed. Lazan's Body Reaching had healed her, but her head was light and her muscles stiff. Leonit's image still hung in her mind, and she fought back tears at the thought of him.

Ten years had passed since an awakened spirit assassinated her father. Ten years since she'd hidden in the cellar, useless, while he died just feet above her. She still had no idea how an awakened could've pierced their estate's spirit-proof glass walls to attack a specific target, and her need for answers ate her alive every waking moment. Even with amber, how could she rebuild her house without vengeance against whoever or whatever had caused this?

The burn scar across her left forearm itched as she swapped shifts, eyeing the raised patches of red that sliced across her pale gray skin. It reminded her every day that not all family was pleasant.

Her younger brother, Gregorzon, had raged against her not long after becoming a Fire Reacher, searing the arm she'd used to protect herself from his firebolt. Their mother had forgiven him. Kasia had not.

Why should I forgive you? she asked him silently as she tugged down her dress's sleeves. *I shan't forgive myself for losing control of my power, and you deserve no better.*

Someone paced outside her tent flaps. Multiple people based on the shadows, so Kasia hastened to put on breeches and a riding dress. In the Reshkan fashion, the light skirt split to reveal her thin legs, and she found it far more practical than Ezmani heavy skirts that made women ride side-saddle or with skirts bunched around them. Her father had been fond of the southern Reshkans anyway, so she considered it a small tribute to him. Even if his acceptance of foreign ways had earned him many rivals.

She skipped braiding her hair, throwing a woolen coat over her narrow shoulders before heading for the tent's entrance. Men like these scouts got grumpy if they were left waiting. If House Uziokaki had gotten involved, then her own mood would be little better.

The dim northern light met her as she stepped into the duskfall morning. She squinted, looking from the nearby campfire to the pair of pacing scouts: Artaxan and Lazan.

"Thank you for your services last night," she said to Lazan with a sharp nod. "I had hoped you wouldn't be needed for healing, but I am grateful you acted swiftly."

Lazan scratched his cleft chin. He was clean shaven like Tazper, and it made him look younger than the other scouts by half a decade. "It was a pleasure, my lady. Besides, healing is my preferred use of my Reaching. It is more refined than brutish strengthening."

She huffed. "There is nothing refined about these woods, but we did not come here for the pleasantries of Kalastok or the rolling countryside. No…" She glanced from Artaxan to a man lingering at the edge of camp, a shortbow hung over his wool coat. He had a scar across his sharp-cut cheek, and he stood with his shoulders rolled forward like a brute ready to fight. "We came for amber, and no Uziokaki is going to stop us."

Tazper rushed over from the fire with his hands stuffed in his pockets. His coat's edges were frayed, and Kasia swore silently she'd get him a new one once they got back—plus, eventually, the Reacher talon he couldn't afford. For all she'd dragged him through, it was the least she owed him.

"That hunter is not happy to see us at all," he rambled, running his hands through his chestnut hair. "He showed up not long after you fainted, swinging a dagger around and claiming we stole the koilee from him. There's an Uziokaki patch on his shoulder, but by the way he was talking, I doubt he is a scion."

"He has no talon, then?" she asked.

Artaxan shook his head.

"Good."

Kasia stepped through them and took a long breath, a hand pressed to her temple. Flashes of her father, then Aliax, danced around her. Their voices joined the screams of those she'd killed to protect Aliax from the attacking lowborn, only to kill him too. She'd Reached so many times in panic. Uncontrollable power coursing through her veins until everything was purple death. They had fallen at her hand, but everyone died in the end.

Except the magnates of the great houses, of course.

"You have the gall to step onto my family's land and threaten my scouts?" she rebuked to the hunter, confirming the Uziokaki sigil of a stag with golden antlers upon his coat. She'd yet to find proof, but she was certain her father's rival house had been part of his assassination. Leonit had made friends and enemies in all corners of Kalastok. The greatest threats, though, were those closest to home.

The hunter crossed his arms. "Your land?"

Kasia stopped less than a stride away. He was taller, reeking of body odor, but she stood straight as a queen as he hunched, her glare tearing into him. "I am Lady Katarzyna, matriarch of House Niezik, and according to the maps commissioned by the Chamber of Scions, you stand on Niezik forestland."

"These aren't your lands." The man spat on her shoe, but took a step back. "Been hunting here all my life. Your pa's maps don't change the hunter's line, and Lord Sazilz said any of you caught crossing it should be reported."

So he knew the truth. Leonit *had* used his influence with the former king, Yaakiin, to redraw the border in Raviak Forest to House Niezik's favor. Yaakiin had been assassinated on the same night as Leonit, which only added to Kasia's suspicions. House Uziokaki had yet to convince the Chamber to revert the border to its original, but they knew well that Kasia and her fallen house had little strength to resist a great house's mercenaries. Intimidation would not work against this man.

"You refer to a hunter's line," she said, hands held behind her back. "What do you mean by that?"

The hunter scoffed. "Of course a high-nosed scion like you wouldn't know. There's old stone markers across the forest, telling hunters which side's yours and which is ours."

Fascinating…

"Very well, then," Kasia said in a conciliatory tone, regret stinging her chest as she eyed the corpse of the koilee nearby. It had not needed to die, but what was done was done. "You desire the koilee, but it attacked us. We killed it, so we deserve our share of the spoils. Let us say this: Do not inform your lords about this encounter, and we will give you a quarter of its pelt."

He hesitated before digging in his heel. "Can't let you take most of my kill. My family needs that money."

Yet he'd considered the offer. Kasia hadn't expected him to accept, as it had been thoroughly unreasonable, but she now had the chance to reach an agreement that was more pleasing to her. "Half-and-half perhaps?" Though she had conceded this was technically

House Uziokaki lands, he couldn't deny they had killed the koilee. Anyone could stalk a beast from a distance.

"Fine," the hunter muttered, holding out his hand. "But if someone asks why I've got only half of it, I ain't lying."

Kasia shook his hand, but let him squeeze far harder than her. He needed to think he'd won. "Very well. Artaxan, have your men split the pelt and meat evenly. Then load it onto his mount." She realized she hadn't asked the man's name, but it didn't matter. House Uziokaki had hundreds of lowborn hunters. This one was nothing but a pawn in their struggle for territory. A pawn, though, could win a war if placed correctly.

Artaxan thumped his chest and ordered the scouts to do as she said. Kasia regretted losing the wealth that came with the pelt, but half was better than nothing. If House Niezik were to push beyond their meager survival through the upcoming everdark and beyond, they would need every kena they could get.

But that hunter's line would be a problem.

Fanzala warmed her hands by the fire with the remaining scouts, and her coffee-brown eyes flicked nervously in Kasia's direction as she approached. "Sorry about the arch, my lady. It was a larger construction than I am used to."

"You did not cause the koilee to attack," Kasia replied, stopping a good distance from the flames. Even there, her scarred arm ached at each *pop* of the logs. "Your… unique… catch stopped me from breaking my back, or worse. It was Harizik's fault I was up there in the first place. Where in the spirits is that coward?"

"On watch," One of the other female scouts, Tania, said from her spot on a downed log. She spoke with a lowborn murmur, her words often merging in ways unaccustomed scions struggled to understand. "Spooked a backbone into that one, the attack did. Good riddance."

Tazper stopped beside Kasia, tipping his wide-brimmed leather hat toward the hunter. "How did it go with him?"

Kasia traced her sharp talon beneath her glove. "He took half the pelt, claiming there is a hunter's line that marks the old border between our lands and theirs. Men like him won't respect a map drawn in Kalastok." Would things have been different if she'd Reached? The hunter could've lied about following the koilee, having just heard the gunshots. "His presence puts our expedition at risk, and I am not confident he won't report us to House Uziokaki."

"Can't we just shoot him?" Tania asked. "They'd do it to us if we were stupid enough to walk into their camp."

"House Uziokaki are as corrupt as any great house," Kasia said, "but this man is just a lowborn hunter. Killing him does nothing to hurt them. If anything, it would just bring us closer to a house war, threatening any claim I have over this amber." She nodded to Fanzala. "You know the area well, so go with Tania to these marker stones and reposition them along my father's redrawn border. Stones like those will require an Earth Reacher to move without leaving evidence behind."

"It's better than sitting around here," Tania replied before waving to Fanzala. "C'mon. We better move quick before we run into another Uziokaki hunter."

"Are you sure deception is the right path?" Fanzala asked, pulling her gloves back on with a regretful glance at the fire. Her short gray curls seemed to burn orange in the glow. "Moving as many boulders as the ones that form such markers will take significant Reaching. I'll need time between each Reach to avoid the Taint."

Tazper leaned closer to Kasia. "She is right, you know. If House Uziokaki discovers we moved the stones, then they will be furious."

"Leaving them means admitting my father lied," Kasia replied, then nodded to Fanzala. "Take the time you need, but do not tarry too long. Koilee aren't the only beasts in these woods."

She considered Fanzala's worry as the Earth Reacher bowed and ran off with Tania to prepare for their journey. Every Reacher feared Realm Taint—the cost of Reaching too often in a short span. Their crystal talons allowed them to pull from another realm, but the First Law of Reaching described the balance that was necessary between the realms: Whatever is taken from one must be returned to it.

Once a talon's energy was exchanged in a Reach, it needed time to refill from Zekiaz's ambient power through the Spirit Crystal. Any additional Reach soon after drew from the Reacher's relevant force. Fire Reachers could never shake off a chill, Water Reachers became eternally dehydrated, and Spirit Reachers lost their sense of self. Because Death Reachers were banned in the Commonwealth, no one had researched how they endured the Taint. Most rumored Death Reachers were either executed or forced to cut off their taloned finger long before they had a chance to become Tainted anyway.

A hand fell on Kasia's shoulder. "You alright, my lady?" Tazper asked, his thin brow raised.

She dropped her head and turned away. "I'm fine."

Across camp, the hunter departed with the koilee fur slung over his horse's back. Kasia imagined raising her hand and striking him down with a blast of Death, but just the thought made her breaths shallow. Memories…

"No!"

She forced her mind to go blank as she gripped her head. Enough pain! Enough hurt! Today was to be her day of victory, when she rooted her house in the amber trade and rebuilt their legacy. The past would haunt her no longer.

Side-eyes met her from every part of the camp as she whistled to Artaxan. "We have lingered here long enough. Lazan has healed me, so there is no reason not to continue."

"It is half-a-day's ride to where we discovered the amber before," the chief scout announced with a signal to break down camp. "Today, we rose as scouts of the house of grain and brew. But tonight, we will sleep as the one bathed in amber!"

The scouts cheered and went to work. Kasia watched them, impressed, as she stopped beside Artaxan and stared up the ledge that had nearly killed her. Amber lay somewhere over it. If she hadn't known better, she would've thought it was a dream. But even dreams didn't come easily nowadays, as nightmares lurked in every shadow.

"That was a fine speech," she said. "Hopefully, the amber deposit you discovered is just as potent."

"It better be," Artaxan replied. "Your family isn't the only one that needs this."

Less than an hour later, they were ready to depart. Tazper helped Kasia mount her horse, and she caught the slightest of grins on his face until she managed to swing her leg over the saddle. She was no stranger to having servants help her. This effort, though, ground more and more against her pride each day. Surely, she should have been halfway decent at this by now?

She stewed in her frustration as Artaxan led them around the slope she'd taken up the hill. Fanzala and Tania headed the opposite direction, sweeping for the border stones. Those were an issue Kasia hadn't accounted for, but she refused to consider the risk any further. They were just hours from her amber. No line of stones would stop her now.

A thick blanket of leaves crunched under-hoof as they passed into the dense patch of half-naked trees that the koilee had emerged from, and the pleasant after-rain smell gave way to the stench of mud and duskfall decay. The forest would soon sleep during the lightless season of everdark. Every day brought less light than the one before it, and with the great light dipping toward the northern horizon, southern valleys left the group in shadow. Artaxan struck a long match and lit his lantern, then passed it back for the others to do the same.

"I am not ready for everdark," Tazper said, lighting his lantern beside Kasia before holding out the match for her to take. "Awakened are frightening enough when you can see them, let alone when they are amid the darkness."

Kasia eyed the match. Her scarred arm seared as the curling smoke met her nose. "No. I can see fine with your lanterns, thank you."

He cocked his head as they climbed a slope, the light falling upon them again. "Are you sure?"

"Yes," she replied curtly. "I learned my lesson with fire years ago."

"Not all fire is shot from your brother's spiteful hand."

She bit her cheek and flexed her taloned hand. "Yet all flames remind me of it. Please, allow me this. You are one of the only people I can trust with my fears, and I ask that you respect them."

Tazper patted the sewn sigil of House Niezik upon his arm—a circle encompassing a triangle with symbols of grain heads, a decorative beer stein, and arrayed playing cards in the gaps between the triangle's edges and the circle's inner border. Leonit had admired the geometric aspects of the design, but all Kasia saw was the businesses that had failed to keep her family prominent. "I am loyal to you and your house, Lady Katarzyna," Tazper said. "It is my responsibility to protect you from what you fear."

"I wouldn't wish that responsibility upon my worst enemy."

They continued in silence for many hours, only the occasional rustling of a hare or other small animal breaking the endless repetition of the horses' hooves striking the ground. The changing of the leaves was beautiful, a sea of warmth amid the shadows, but Kasia grew tenser by the minute. And she'd already been wound tighter than her mother during one of her episodes.

"How much further?" she shouted ahead to Artaxan, who stopped alongside a stream to refill his canteen. Its flow would lead to the Ty River that wound past her family's town of Tystok. Her body ached for home's comforts, but her heart panged at the thought of returning to a mother and brother who hated her.

"Not more than five miles by the flight of the raven," Artaxan said with a swig.

Kasia didn't join the others at the stream-side. Dismounting would be an embarrassing waste of time and effort, so she gave Tazper a smile as he took her canteen. Ravens fluttered through the trees, *caw*-ing down at the intruding scouts. When one flew over Kasia, it revealed a tuft of orange on its chest.

"What are those birds called?" she asked Laxkal, a tall scout who stood apart from the others. "I have never seen a raven with color before."

He scratched his ragged brown beard and shrugged his shoulders that were twice as wide as her own. "Aren't you the one in charge? What do you want them to be called?"

Another scout shook her head and pointed up at the nearest one. "Can't you tell? They're amber-throated ravens. It's probably a good omen that we're close."

"There are no such things as omens," Kasia said, taking back her canteen from Tazper, but she couldn't deny that the ravens were beautiful. That splash of color seemed to scream through their black feathers and proclaim their presence. A challenge to all nearby predators. "We rise and fall by our actions and those of our enemies."

Some of the other scouts aimed their rifles. The first shot cracked through the woods, scattering the birds as the men laughed.

"Stop!" Kasia commanded. "You lot left a koilee orphaned with those guns. Shoot a bird that small, and all you'll have are feathers in return for your spent ammunition." She snapped her gaze to Artaxan. "Are we finished here?"

He took another swig before wiping his mouth with his sleeve. "We can be. Mount up! We've got more amber in the ground than on bird throats."

There better be.

Despite the shots, the flock kept with the scouts as they rode northeast. Avian chattering turned to pleasant songs that hung among the clouds. If Kasia had believed in omens, she'd have said they were showing the way to the amber she sought, but she held no such hope. The practical explanation was that the birds had learned to eat scraps of bread dropped by hunters. Still, they lifted a small weight off her shoulders.

Nearly two hours passed before Artaxan pointed to a willow grove in the valley below. "It's just ahead," he said. "We could only take a bag full last time, but I promise there's more."

Kasia pushed her horse into a labored trot, but it resisted after days of long journeys. Or she was doing it wrong. Either way, they slowed to a walk once again, grinding her already worn patience to its end.

"I could run faster than this," she grumbled to Tazper beside her.

He held out his arms. "But that would ruin the moment! You must take a moment to at least look at this view. The great light is hitting the forest perfectly, as if it were ablaze in gold."

"Perhaps I should commission you as my painter instead of my footman."

"I would not recommend it," he said. "Painting takes a steady hand, and my mother says I mix up my greens with my grays."

She narrowed her eyes, trying to imagine what it would be like for the forest to be as gray as her hair. "Why did you not mention this before? I have never heard of such a condition."

He slumped in his saddle. "Your estate lacks vibrant greens, so it did not come up in conversation."

"As long as you can see amber, then we will have no issues," she said with a fake smile. Her nerves were too frayed to muster a real one.

"There!" Lazan exclaimed from their left flank, sweeping his horse to a divot in the earth before dismounting.

Kasia followed the Body Reacher. He threw aside his long coat, his muscles bulging through his shirt beneath as he dug furiously. She'd heard of Body Reachers enhancing people's strength for labor, but had rarely seen it until now. No one joined him. Much in the same way that one did not interfere with a knight's charge, they would only get in the way of a man with that much power.

Lazan rose moments later with a yellow-orange rock clutched in his fist. While technically not a mineral or gem, it held a similar shimmer that stole Kasia's breath. Amber of the purest make. Most would be underground, so if there were chunks this large on the surface, surely there would be plenty to sell.

"We did it!" Kasia gasped, throwing herself off her horse and stumbling toward Lazan. "It is actually here."

He held out the piece of amber for her to take. "You sponsored this journey. Take its first—"

BANG!

An object whizzed past Kasia's face. Her ears rang as blood splattered over her coat. The scouts raised their guns, but she could only stare at the mangled remnants of Lazan's right hand.

"Put down your rifles!" a gruff voice called over the grove. "I would happily take the excuse to put a bullet into your lady's head."

RAVEN BLOOD

Kasia's cold breaths caught in her throat. Out of instinct alone, she grabbed Lazan's forearm to keep him from falling, but the blood…

"You're no stranger to death," Aliax whispered in her head.

"He's not dead yet," she replied.

Her words cut the tense silence that hung over the grove like a veil. Artaxan's scouts had yet to lower their weapons, and when she found the chief scout among the foliage, he was looking at her for instruction.

They'll shoot us all.

That realization tore her from her trance enough for her to mutter a command. "Lower your guns."

She stared again at Lazan's shot right hand, barely recognizable as a limb at all. The scouts' grumbled protests, though, required no sight to understand. They were afraid. Why lower their weapons and leave themselves defenseless against whatever bandits had found them?

"Lower your guns!" Kasia repeated, her voice savage and raw.

The scouts complied as she helped Lazan to the ground. Her head spun from the blood that covered them both. She'd seen Death from her Reaching, but it was more like a decay that swept over their body. This… She'd only heard stories of such disfigurement from commanders who'd visited Leonit to petition for his support.

But Lazan showed no such panic. He bared his teeth, guiding her arm away. "Deal with the attackers, my lady," he said. "A Body Reacher must be prepared to heal any wound, even his own."

She nodded absently as he bit the glove over his left, taloned hand and ripped it free. Deep red wisps rose from the gray crystal over his index finger, drifting toward his injured hand. Bones and skin grew from nothing. They reformed exactly what his hand had looked like before, but the process was gruesome to watch, so Kasia stood and scanned the woods for their attackers.

Men dressed in oak-brown lined the ridge ahead. Their buttoned uniforms were too fine for lowborn hunters, and they wore tall yellow hats with chin straps and silver-crafted fronts. No, these were no bandits.

They were Uziokaki mercenaries.

A grim-faced man of middle age stepped from behind their line, a cigar dangling from his fingers and ash leaking from its end. He wore a similar jacket and hat to his mercenaries, but his golden buttons were undone and tight marksman's gloves clung to his hands. Two chains—one of gold and another of glass—ran across the front of his jacket, jangling as he walked. Such decorative uses of expensive spirit-repelling glass were unheard of outside the most powerful houses.

"Lady Katarzyna," the man said in a voice oozing with contempt. "What brings you so deep into my house's lands with armed scouts, stealing from our resources?"

"May I ask with whom I speak?" Kasia shouted, unable to hold back her temper. Leonit wouldn't have been pleased, but even he had admitted that one must bare their fangs when threatened. "You have fired upon my Reacher, a *scion*, and I shall not tolerate such violence!"

The man huffed, then took a puff from his cigar. "I am Lord Razamat of House Uziokaki, commander of the Third Company of the Raven Regiment and protector of Raviak Forest. Now, must I repeat myself?"

Kasia sneered. "You Uziokaki are quite fond of your voices, so why not?"

"You truly are Leonit's daughter."

"Which means I am matriarch of House Niezik, while you are a distant cousin of Lord Sazilz of your own house." She garnered her will and banished the fear from her voice. "As such, you will show me respect as you tread on *my* lands."

Razamat flicked his cigar into a nearby bush, its smoke curling through the naked twigs. "Best be careful when you use words like that, girl."

Kasia glanced over her shoulder as footsteps approached from behind. Lazan had his arm over Tazper's shoulder, limping despite his hand being completely healed—only possible for a Body Reacher within a day of the injury.

"Do not choose a fight on my behalf, my lady," Lazan said.

"I had no intention to," she replied quietly. "This fight was my father's, now mine."

She advanced up the hill, staring down the mercenaries. The barrels of their guns glinted in the light, and she imagined the bullets within flying toward her faster than she could blink. They would do worse than mangle her hand. These were trained soldiers with flintlock rifles, far more accurate than old muskets. They could shoot her in the head and heart before her body registered what had happened. One moment, she would be climbing toward Razamat, and the next, her spirit would fall from her body.

A cool breeze carried over the ridge as she stopped two strides from Razamat. He wasn't an ugly man, besides a scabbed-over rash that ducked beneath his left collar, and he smelt of dawnrise lavender, not the odor of Artaxan and his unwashed scouts.

She held out her gloved hand to shake. Her Death Reaching was a secret, but among scions, it was considered a threat to remove one's gloves. Most Realm Reaching could be used as a weapon in the right context.

"Let us speak like the scions we are instead of shouting across this motherforsaken grove," she said. "Both of our houses have claims to this contested land, so is it not better for us to work out a deal than start another war between us? The Commonwealth has enough issues without us tearing it apart."

"Perhaps you are more than you appear," Razamat said with an amused smirk, as she'd hoped. It was unlikely that Fanzala had moved all the border stones yet, and negotiations would be difficult until she had that leg to stand on. "Very well, let us negotiate."

He shook her hand far harder than necessary, but his smirk vanished as she matched his intensity. They stood there for a moment, hands clasped in a silent duel until he released her and whistled to his mercenaries. "Set up my command tent in the valley, and bring our finest beer for the matriarch."

Kasia tilted up her chin. "Lead the way, Lord Razamat."

Her scouts moved aside as the mercenaries moved a horse-drawn cart from the far end of the hill, then went to work building the tent. Both factions' scouts grumbled. Even among the lowborn, bad blood was rampant between houses Niezik and Uziokaki, and any of them would take any chance to knock their foes down a notch. Kasia was no different. She knew, though, when she was outgunned. Leonit had taught her well that only a fool fired with no hope of victory.

"Your people look exhausted," Razamat said, leaning on a beer barrel as he admired the tent poles. It was a far larger construction than Kasia's measly tent, and hers dwarfed those of her scouts. "Why rush if you claim this land is yours?"

Kasia examined his broad shoulders and muscled arms beneath his coat. This was a commander, not a lazy scion of the gentry. "Sloth of the body spreads to the mind. We made a discovery and sought to take advantage of it before the Ephemeral Storms flood this forest. I assume that is why you are here as well?"

"A fair reason enough." He waved to a nearby mercenary, who brought two wooden goblets and filled them from the barrel. Glass ones were far too expensive and fragile to drink from outside the great house estates. "Care to enjoy a drink with me while we wait for the brutes to finish their labor? I must admit, it is not as fine as that you would find in Kalastok, but it does the job."

She took one of the goblets, hiding her reluctance behind a grateful smile. Drink and smoke alike were fine tools to dull one's mind, but she much preferred only dulling her opponent's.

"Take a sip when others down their own," Leonit had told her when she'd held her first drink as a young girl. *"Pretend you are more intoxicated than you are, and a man will tell you of every spirit in his closet."*

So she sipped the bitter beer. Razamat had not lied about it being far from the finest, and it took all her strength not to sneer down at the dark liquid. Luckily, the Uziokaki lord was not so temperate. He finished his goblet in a few long swigs, then wiped his dripping lip with his sleeve. From the stain across his woolen coat, it was not the first time he'd done so, and Kasia betted it wouldn't be the last either.

"You may have another," she insisted with another sip. "While you drink, I may present my proposal based on the maps provided by the king's secretaries."

Razamat showed no hesitation to refill his goblet from the spigot. "Hah! Those arrogant fools? I would be surprised if any of them had stepped foot in Raviak Forest for two centuries."

"Perhaps…" She stayed her tongue until the tent was ready. Her evidence required a table to present convincingly. "Do not believe that I failed to notice your evasion. You have not explained yet why you find yourself so deep in the forest."

"Neither have you, but I assume it has to do with whatever your Body Reacher was holding."

Kasia took another sip. "It was nothing, unfortunately."

But she couldn't hide her spite behind the goblet. Leonit would've told her to reveal a grain of truth to conceal her lie. She couldn't—not when everything she'd worked for was on the line. This amber was *hers*, and spirits be damned if she would allow a Uziokaki to take it.

"And just when I thought we were being cordial," Razamat replied, tipping his goblet side to side, "you remind me that you are the matriarch of a house of snakes. Spirit-damn, girl, you remind me of my daughter. She is half your age with no less spite."

"You'd see through a lie like that," Aliax said in her head. *"Why'd you think he wouldn't?"*

Kasia bit her cheek, but before she had the chance to reply, one of the mercenaries approached. The tent was finished.

At Razamat's signal, the mercenary saluted and stepped aside, allowing the scion lord to push past the tent's flap. Kasia pulled a rolled-up canvas from her horse's saddle bag before following. The guards on either side of the entrance gave her a distrusting look—one which she mirrored. Artaxan's scouts positioned themselves on the western edge of the camp, but they would be too far to stop an assault within the tent. She would be alone the moment she stepped inside.

Except she had a weapon greater than any mercenary's gun.

Fifteen feet long and wide, the tent easily fit a round table, chairs, and another rectangular table with writing supplies on it. The mercenaries had laid out a pair of patterned rugs that covered most of the space. They were boring, using Uziokaki browns and forest greens, and sucked the duskfall light out of the space. A few lanterns hanging from the tentpoles lit it enough, though, for writing to be legible. Just as Kasia needed.

"You mentioned before that the king's secretaries never visit these woods," she said, taking the seat Razamat offered her. A serving girl waited for her to sit before bringing out bread and sliced apples for them. Kasia plucked one slice from the plate and dangled it from her fingers as she continued, "My father, however, toured beneath these trees many times. He knew well which lands were ours, and he ensured the king knew the same."

"A foreign king," Razamat spat.

"Reshkan-born, yes, yet elected by the Chamber of Scions all the same." She bit the apple, and savored its juices that covered the beer's bitter aftertaste. "You would not dare deny that he had legal authority over such matters, would you?"

Razamat drank the rest of his goblet, then held it out for the serving girl to take. Any amusement in his voice vanished. "You are playing a dangerous game. Yaakiin is not king anymore, and King Jazuk would not take kindly to fraud between our houses."

Kasia scoffed. "Fraud is as common among the great houses as bastards. But you are a father who understands the importance of order. It is good, then, that what I bring is not fraud, but legitimate government documents bearing King Yaakiin's seal."

She pushed the food to Razamat's end of the table before unfurling her canvas map and laying it between them. It showed the entirety of Raviak Forest and the outlying villages. The antlered raven of House Uziokaki filled the space on the eastern edge, while House Niezik's enclosed triangle lay to the west. Between them, a twisting line cut through the woods to mark the border between the houses' lands—or, at least, the line Leonit had convinced the deceased king of.

Razamat tore a piece of bread in half and stuffed it in his mouth, speaking as he chewed. "A map drawn without House Uziokaki's approval. It means nothing."

Kasia drummed her fingers on the table. What would it take to convince this bullheaded man she was right? If a king's seal was not enough, Fanzala's shifted stones would have to be.

"Millions have died over the centuries because of lines on a map," Kasia replied. "The Keloshan Empire often draws one across our eastern lands, yet it means nothing if our king does not approve. How are you any different?"

"You said you had a proposal," Razamat grunted. "Give it, or leave. I grow tired of your insistence on these untruths."

Kasia tapped their current location on the map, west of her father's border. "In return for your acceptance of our lands as designated by the king, I am willing to grant House Uziokaki a significant discount on any resources we extract from Raviak Forest. You would gain even greater control over the fur, meat, and forestry trades. Buy from us, then use the goods or sell them at a profit. You gain without needing to devote any workers to the effort."

"So this includes any of your amber yield, then?"

She dug her finger into the map. *Fuck you!*

Razamat took another goblet of beer and sat back, crossing his legs. "Did you believe me to be blind? A hunter came to my men with claims of Niezik scouts, so I knew you were searching for something valuable. Why else would a matriarch stray this far into the dense woods? When I saw that amber piece in your Reacher's hand, I knew it was what you had come for. *That* is far more valuable than fur and mother-damned wood!"

"And it will be mine," Kasia snapped as she dug her gloved fingers into the table's edge. "It was *my* scouts who discovered the amber on *my* land. Check the hunters' border markers if you don't believe me."

Time was up. She bit her cheek, knowing Fanzala probably was still yet to finish. All she could hope for now was that Razamat would rather rest for the evening than ride through the night to check the stones.

The commander gulped down the beer and slammed the goblet on the table. Then he stood and tugged on his military jacket. "We know the marker stones well, as all Uziokaki hunters do. Let us ride to them tomorrow, and I will show you myself that your ridiculous line does not match reality. The amber is House Uziokaki's. You are trespassing, and I will ensure the tale of Leonit Niezik's deceitful spawn is heard throughout the Commonwealth."

Kasia sneered. Leonit would've kept his calm, swirling his own goblet in amusement, but Razamat's mockery dug deep into her nerves. "Speak ill of my father again, and you won't have a tongue to spread any tales with."

She stormed out of the tent. Another moment with him, and she was convinced she'd have Reached. His mercenaries would react to such an attack, though, revealing her as a Death Reacher. No one else could know. The rumors about Aliax's death would only grow, and every shred of prestige her family had left would be lost.

Tazper awaited her outside, having to jog just to keep up with her. "Err, my lady, is all well?"

"What do you think?"

He cleared his throat. "He did not agree to concede to your father's border, then?"

"No, but I expected that." She stopped with a sigh, forcing her stray hair behind her ears. Artaxan and the other scouts had set up their tents while she was with Razamat, and the chief scout paced outside her tent. But she wasn't ready to face him yet. "Razamat mocked my father," she admitted. "Leonit knew when to tell a veiled lie, yes, but he was more than that. He was more than the Reshkan-lover they call him now. Without him, we'd still be enduring the glass shortage that plagued the beginnings of King Yaakiin's reign. We lost lands to the three empires, but we'd have faced war on every front if he hadn't convinced Yaakiin to negotiate!"

"Sometimes people wish to fight," Tazper said with a shrug, "even if it is futile. You are willing to struggle for every inch of the land Leonit claimed in this forest, so can you blame others when the Reduction Treaties stole much of the Commonwealth's lands with a stroke of a quill?"

Flames burned in Kasia's eyes. "My fight is *not* futile."

"Nor do I believe it is, but it is reasonable to accept that not everyone agreed with Leonit. His fascination with other nations probably gave him insights into the world. Maybe they also made him vulnerable when the nations he admired turned on him."

Kasia turned away and waved a dismissive hand. "Your services are not needed for the rest of the night."

"Very well." He bowed his head, then started toward his tent, but he stopped after a few strides. "Kasia, I want the best for you and this house—we all do. Just… Leonit may have been more than what people say he was, but so, too, are you more than his daughter. Your legacy as matriarch is yours to write. Not many of us get the chance to choose our own path."

She considered that for a moment. Of course, he was right that she was privileged to be the matriarch of a significant family, but House Niezik had fallen from their place among the great houses. Kasia was scorned for her father's actions. Right or not, it didn't matter. Her path had been paved the moment that awakened entered their estate. Her duty was to rebuild her house and avenge her father.

Amber would bring her closer to the former, but the latter was a mountain she'd yet to find, let alone climb. Whether she succeeded would determine her legacy. Nothing else.

"Thank you, Tazper," she said, relenting out of exhaustion. It had been another long day, and arguing with her friend would get her nowhere. "Now get some rest. We ride for the hunters' marks tomorrow."

They each headed toward their tent, and Kasia steeled herself as Artaxan held his hands behind his back, head bowed. "What's the status, my lady?" he asked.

She nodded toward the mercenaries across the grove. "Razamat will only be convinced if the hunters' marks prove the border is where my father said."

"You're confident Fanzala is done, then?"

"No, but since my other choices were a shootout or conceding that the land is theirs, I chose to risk it." She winced. To succeed Fanzala and Tania would have to push their horses even harder than they had already, and Fanzala would have to Reach often. Kasia had no intent to inflict Realm Taint on her. If it was the difference between the amber being theirs or House Uziokaki's, though, surely the Earth Reacher would accept a hefty sum of keni in exchange for a bit of Taint?

Artaxan held a fist to his chest. "Then I'm sure she'll do the job. She and Tania were determined to make you proud when they left."

She smiled. "All of you have made this possible. House Uziokaki may have interfered, but we are here, standing above who knows how much amber, because of you and your scouts. I *am* proud. But pride cannot pay my family's debts. Once we come out of this as victors, both our prides and coin purses will be heavier than a magnate's gut."

"I hope so, my lady."

OF STONE AND PAPER

Kasia awoke the next morning to rain pattering on her tent's canvas. She'd slept at an odd angle, and her neck cracked as she stretched. Spirits, she was sore. Artaxan had not lied about the stresses the body endured after riding on horseback for so many days.

It would be over soon if she could prove to Razamat that she was right. Fanzala had moved most, if not all, of the border stones by now. At least, that's what Kasia told herself to stop nerves from creeping over her. Any sign of fear would lend favor to Razamat's doubts, so she would show him none.

A cough came from outside the tent.

"What is it, Tazper?" she asked with a groan. He'd been her footman so long that even coughs were familiar now. Everyone had certain *unique* aspects about them, and Tazper… well… he had many identifying factors.

"Lord Razamat and his mercenaries await us," he replied. "They seem quite irritated."

Kasia cursed to herself. "Fine. Give me a moment."

She put on her riding dress and breeches, then snatched her long woolen coat, flipping up the collar as she clambered into the duskfall morning. Clouds covered overhead. The great light, though, rested at the horizon, and its rays made each raindrop twinkle before striking her head with an unwelcome chill.

"Is Artaxan planning to send everyone?" she asked Tazper. "We should leave a pair of scouts behind to ensure House Uziokaki doesn't play any tricks."

He held out his wide-brimmed hat. "You should keep the rain off your head. We cannot have you getting ill on such an important expedition."

She shook her head and headed toward the southern edge of the camp, where the horses were tied up. The scouts and mercenaries were already gathered. "I appreciate the offer, but there is no need. Water ruining my hair is the least of my concerns this morn'." In truth, she had her own hat, but it was a noble woman's, more for fashion than function. Getting it wet would just make a chore for her few remaining servants upon her return, and she couldn't afford to replace luxuries until they secured the amber.

Razamat noticed their approach and stomped over. With his jacket unbuttoned, he already had water coating the front of his shirt. At least his ridiculous hat managed to keep some of the water off his deeply wrinkled brow as he grumbled at Kasia.

"This is why the wilderness is not the place for house heads! You lot are too used to waking when you choose and dawdling all day. I will not stand for such a delay as you waste time on House Uziokaki lands."

Kasia gave a shallow curtsy. "My apologies, Lord Razamat. I had not realized that I had commanded you to stand. Certainly, one of your men has a chair or perhaps a fallen log for you to sit on?"

One of her scouts snorted from nearby, but silenced at a glare from Razamat. "If you wish to be treated like a matriarch, then act like it," he said. "Otherwise I will treat you like my insolent daughter. I endure this search for the hunters' border stones out of a desire to avoid civil war between our houses. You should thank me for my restraint." He threw his foot into his horse's stirrup, then swept up into the saddle with far more dexterity than seemed possible.

Kasia did her best to emulate the motion, but nearly slid off the other side as she mounted. Only a well-timed snatch by Tazper prevented her from falling into the muck.

"Thank you," she mouthed to him before regaining her posture. Not that it did much. Her riding seat still resembled a sack of grain, and Razamat surely noticed.

The Uziokaki scion took the lead, heading in the direction of Leonit's claimed border. Even a single marker being there would lend credence to Kasia's arguments, and she held onto hope that he wouldn't notice if there were some missing. Artaxan ruined it.

"Harizik was near the edge of camp," he whispered, "and he noticed a couple mercenaries riding northeast. No doubt, they're headed to check if any stones remain on the old border."

Kasia clenched her legs tighter against her horse, accidentally pushing it into a trot until she managed to bring it back under control. Her cheeks burned as Razamat's men smirked back at her.

"At least Harizik's reclusiveness was useful for once," she said to Artaxan. "This could complicate things."

Artaxan huffed. "Has anything been simple so far? Why would the route ahead be any different?"

They continued over rolling hills and through leaf-littered deer trails for another hour until they neared Leonit's claimed border. Not long later, a scout shouted, pointing to their right.

A boulder rose from beside a creek whose flow was little more than a trickle. House Niezik's emblem had been carved into the visible, western side of it, and a mercenary rode to confirm House Uziokaki's was on the other. No rocks like it were anywhere near, but the ground appeared undisturbed. Fanzala had done her work well. Razamat, though, frowned back at Kasia.

"This stone is not natural," he said.

She shrugged. "Our houses both have plenty of Reachers in our employ. It is not inconceivable that one placed these markers many years ago."

"How many Reachers does he have?" Aliax said in her head. *"You came prepared, but did he?"*

Kasia studied the gathered mercenaries as Razamat replied, but his words were lost to her. Aliax was right. Any of the mercenaries could be Reachers, and she'd not considered that before. Their numbers alone were enough of a threat. Though Razamat would obviously be a Reacher as a scion of a great house, any others with him could take the situation from difficult to impossible. Especially a Truth Reacher.

But if Razamat had another Reacher, none showed talons beneath their tight marksmen gloves. He was an insignificant cousin of Uziokaki patriarch Sazilz, so they had likely decided not to waste Reachers on his forest patrol. Razamat had not revealed which realm he was bound to himself, but Spirit Reachers were by far the most common. Kasia took heart that he didn't know she had an Earth Reacher to move the stones.

A hand fell on her shoulder.

"Lord Razamat wishes to check for another," Tazper said, his touch and tone both gentle.

Kasia met Razamat's stern gaze. "Of course. Let us not dally in this muck then. We have more markers that you *insist* on finding."

They repeated the search for much of the day, Kasia relaxing more with each marker they found on or near Leonit's border along the stream. Razamat's anger grew with each. By the time Kasia's mechanical watch ticked to the sixteenth of their twenty-hour day, they had found four, and Razamat spent most of his time berating a mercenary with silver epaulets on her uniform's shoulders.

The fifth marker awaited them beneath a weeping willow, its branches hanging over the boulder and drifting across the emblems on each side. It was the kind of tree that commanded an area for twenty feet each direction, all other beings besides moss, fungi, and the smallest of ants respecting its space. Razamat held no such respect.

"Fuck!" he yelled into the duskfall sky.

The silver mercenary sought to calm him, but Razamat held no patience. He drew his single-shot pistol and pulled back the hammer before firing into the Niezik emblem.

Kasia covered her ears too slowly. Her ears rang from the blast as the sharp smell of gunpowder stung her nostrils. Each time she blinked, she remembered sitting beneath her father's trap door, his futile shot at the attacking awakened thundering through the house. He'd fallen to the floor with a hollow *thud* moments later, and part of her had died with him.

"That's enough, Lord Razamat," she insisted. "I have proven my point, and you have obviously lost your temper. Let us return to camp before a bullet ends up in one of our heads."

Razamat pointed the gun at her, but she did not flinch. He wanted her afraid. They all wanted her afraid. Her fear had been claimed long ago, though, and no man with a pistol would change that.

"This is not over!" he said, his face contorted with rage. "I will uncover your deceit, Katarzyna."

She turned her horse about, glancing from his gun to him. "Are we finished here?"

Two approaching riders interrupted Razamat before he could reply. They burst through the willow from the west, wearing the uniforms of Uziokaki mercenaries. The first of them held his fist over his heart as he bowed to Razamat.

"My lord, we scouted the old border for any signs of disturbances or markers," he said. "There appeared to be none, but when we doubled back, we found a smaller, moss-covered marker bearing the Uziokaki and Niezik emblems. The others may have been moved, with this one being missed."

Damn it all.

Kasia drew her own pistol, aiming at Razamat. Any shot with her inexperienced hand would be unlikely to hit him at this distance, but the threat would give him pause. "Your men question my honor!"

Razamat scoffed. "There is no honor in your house to question. It is over, girl. You had the stones moved, didn't you?"

"Or your scouts lied. Awfully convenient, is it not, that they arrived here now?"

The silver mercenary rode between them, a hand held toward each of them. "Do not leave your daughter fatherless over a line," she said to Razamat before looking at Kasia. "We found your lie, Lady Katarzyna. You seem a smart enough matriarch to understand this won't end in your favor."

"I will not allow my honor to be questioned," Kasia replied. "Lord Razamat of House Uziokaki, I challenge you to a duel to settle the question of the border between our houses' lands. If you so boldly believe I have deceived you, then face me."

Tazper gasped. "What are you doing?"

"This is not a wise approach," Artaxan added. "Lord Razamat is a marksman!"

"Do you accept?" Kasia said, ignoring her allies' pleas. Duels were an unconventional but not illegal way to settle disputes among scions. Usually, each duelist had a Body Reacher to heal what injuries occurred. She bet that Razamat didn't.

The fear in the silver mercenary's eyes confirmed her suspicions, but Razamat grinned. "Very well," he said. "I have no desire to see you dead, but you may have your duel."

THE AMBER DUEL

The cool eastern breeze blew stray strands of ashen hair into Kasia's face as she stood beneath the weeping willow. Amber-throated ravens fluttered overhead, their calls echoing over the stream as Artaxan, Tazper, and Lazan alike tried to convince Kasia to back down from her challenge. But she didn't listen to their appeals.

Instead, she traced her family's sigil on the border stone and wondered what her father would've done. The lowest branches graced her sleeves, making her wince at their touch along her scarred forearm. It itched more than stung. She'd learned not to scratch it, though, as remembering those who'd hurt her was better than feeling nothing. Why remove the motivation that pushed her ever forward?

"Father wouldn't have allowed his plan to be discovered," she said, interrupting Tazper. He held her forearm, but her glare sent him reeling. "But he would have fought for every piece of ground he claimed."

"That may have killed him in the end," Tazper replied.

"Then I'll avenge him."

Lazan shook his head, his now healed hand held behind his back. "Vengeance does not bring fullness, my lady. Lord Razamat may have shot me, but I would rather us all leave her alive than with blood on our hands."

Kasia touched her pistol, holstered at her hip. "You are afraid of blood on your hands? Fine. Then it is well and good that you won't be the one to pull the trigger."

She glanced between the men to Razamat. The silver mercenary pushed her finger into his chest, red-faced, but he stood defiantly. No scion as proud as him would stand down from a challenge against a rival house. Unfortunately, he would have better aim than her, and she remembered his mention of a daughter. Winning could leave the girl like her.

"You have never been shot before," Artaxan told her. "It is unlikely you will have any blood on your hands but your own when this is over."

Kasia nodded. "That is why I need Lazan's help."

"How, my lady?" the Reacher asked. "I can heal you once the duel is over, but besides that…"

"Can you not enhance a person's strength?"

Tazper grabbed her shoulders. "Please telling me you are not *planning* to get shot?"

"I am inexperienced with a pistol compared to him," Kasia replied, tolerating his grip for now. She'd have done so for no one else, but his intentions were to help, as always. "It is likely I will miss when he does not, so I must be able to endure beyond the first round. Once he is thoroughly injured, I will offer Lazan's services to heal us both in return for him conceding."

"That would require a second Reach in a short span," Lazan said, arms crossed.

Kasia brushed Tazper away with a reassuring smile. "Precisely why I propose that we double your payment for this journey. Once the amber is secure, such a fee will be little hassle for me." She hated asking such a sacrifice of him, but this was her only chance. If they lost this amber, she would never have the funds to fund her vengeance.

"Triple," Lazan insisted. "I'm not enduring Realm Taint without good pay. Every bit of it I get takes time off my body's lifespan, and unlike the great house magnates, I don't get another life."

"Fine." She pulled up her right sleeve. "Hurry, before he notices."

The marker stone and drooping willow branches offered plenty of cover as Lazan touched his crystal talon to her wrist. He Reached, and a chill rushed up her arm as red spiraled from his hand. It enveloped her arm, then shot into her veins. Energy came with it.

Kasia stepped back with the longest breath she'd ever taken. Her lungs sucked in the air greedily, able to hold more as colors grew so vivid that her eyes ached. But it was more a tickle than pain, and her soreness vanished. Each of her senses exploded and dulled at the same time, as if enhanced but less sensitive.

It was intoxicating.

"Spirits!" she exclaimed before catching herself and lowering her voice. "Lazan, how have you never shown me this?"

He half-turned away, his head drooping. "I can heal for an extended time with a single Reach, but fortifying someone's body takes all the energy immediately. It is also known to be addicting for the receiver."

She unholstered her revolver. It was well made and had been a significant weight in her hand before, but now, it felt no heavier than a feather. "I see why."

"Do not ask me to do this again, my lady. I fear what addiction to such magic could do to you."

Tazper nodded. "You are the strongest person I know already. Relying on Reaching will only make you vulnerable."

"Listen to them," Aliax said in her head.

"If all are in alignment," Kasia replied, "then I won't contest it, for now."

"We also agree that you should not duel in the first place," Tazper said.

Kasia chuckled and stepped past him with what should've been a light pat on the shoulder. It sent him staggering back, rubbing where she'd hit. "It is alright to be wrong sometimes."

Her steps were fluid, light as Razamat noticed her advance. "Have you found your senses?" he asked. "Or have you decided that dueling a trained marksman is a sound action."

"I am ready," she replied, stopping in an open strip between the trees. A raven's objection answered from above, but she focused only on her foe. "Tazper will be my second."

"I will be?" Tazper asked before coughing and standing up straighter. "I meant that I, of course, will be your second. Does that not mean it is my responsibility to attempt reconciliation?"

"No. Just pace the distance and check the gun."

Razamat handed his pistol to the silver mercenary and signaled for her to mirror Tazper. Despite having no Reachers among his ranks to save his life, he showed no fear. Either confidence or complacence could cause such a thing, and Kasia hoped it was the latter.

When the paces were marked, each second relinquished the pistols and stepped back. Kasia never took her eye off Razamat. He wasn't the lord of his house, but he represented those who'd opposed her father. They had profited greatly off House Niezik's downfall, and she would see that they suffered for every kena they'd earned in his wake.

"Fire on my signal," the silver mercenary said, holding up a hand.

Kasia raised her revolver and held it with two hands. Lazan had granted her increased strength, but Razamat needed to believe she struggled with the recoil. The mercenary captain himself needed only a single hand around his gun's handle. While Kasia swayed with each breath, he stood still as stone.

"Fire!"

The order caught Kasia off guard. She sucked in a breath just as the silver mercenary spoke, and the *CRACK* of Razamat's shot struck her ears before she pulled the trigger.

She fought the revolver as it yanked toward the sky. Her grip held, and she silently thanked Lazan for his Reaching. From Razamat's raised chin, though, she'd missed badly. At least he hadn't...

A wet tightness struck her stomach, but she felt no pain as she took one hand from the gun and held it over her naval. Still, she refused to look away from Razamat. The warm liquid that met her fingers required no sight to identify. And the distant throb in her head told her something was wrong. Her body had been fortified, but a bullet wound was a bullet wound.

Fuck.

Panic squeezed her throat. Even without the pain, she'd never been shot before. Gregorzon's flames had seared her skin and sent her screaming to the ground, but knowing that a metal bullet had plunged through her core was far more terrifying. Lazan's Reaching would only last so long. Then, the death she was so familiar with would claw for her to join its realm.

Razamat lowered his gun. "You have taken a wound, Lady Katarzyna," he said, his voice distant as the gunshots still echoed in her ears. "Signal to your Body Reacher, and let us be done with this game."

"This isn't worth dying for, my love," Aliax pleaded. *"You have a life to live for more than amber and riches. Don't waste it for pride now."*

Kasia sucked in a sharp breath. Her aim had drifted downward in her shock, so she thrust the gun toward him, jaw clenched as she pulled back the hammer.

"This is not finished!" she screamed, but her hand trembled. "I am not dead!"

"I do not wish for your death," Razamat said. "This is folly! You are but a young woman with much of life to see."

But Kasia just threw her free hand toward the silver mercenary. "Another round. Now!"

The throbbing spread from her head to the wound itself. Not enough to force her down, but it was a constant reminder of her initial failure. Another round meant another shot. He would not miss. If she did, what hope was there of winning the duel?

"My lord," the silver mercenary protested. "There is no reason for this to continue."

Razamat sighed. "She has her rights by the letter of the law to continue until death. If I stand down, then victory is hers."

"Start!" Kasia shouted, turning her gun on the silver mercenary.

The woman rolled her eyes. "It's your death. Fire on my signal."

Razamat shook his head as Kasia aimed at him again. All she needed was a solid hit on a major organ. How hard could that be?

She took a long breath this time, holding it as Razamat finally raised his gun again. His eyes seemed hollow, and his mouth now curved downward like a disappointed father. He did not waver.

"Fire!"

Instincts answered before Kasia could even think. Her revolver shot back against her single hand this time, but she held firm as the bullet burst free, the smell of gunpowder burning through her brain. The world went silent beyond the high-pitched ringing in her ears. All she saw was Razamat and the puff of shredded leaves that fell from the tree behind him.

Another miss.

She cursed her aim as she looked away, finding Tazper just strides away. Tears wettened his eyes. But she didn't follow his gaze. Her dulled senses said she'd been shot in the left shoulder, and she couldn't move that arm. It was mere inches from her heart. A miss for a marksman, and she had no doubt he could've killed her with ease.

Tazper rushed to her. "Kasia? Kasia, are you alright?"

"What does it look like?" she spat, biting her cheek so hard she tasted blood. What did a bit more matter? She'd bleed out soon anyway. Her plan had failed, and all she could do was fire once more in blind hope of a hit. If not...

"I don't wish for you to join me," Aliax said. *"You can't talk to me if you're gone."*

"Enough!" Razamat demanded, his arms held out. "Please, Katarzyna, show some sense. Is amber truly worth all this suffering?"

Kasia swung her gun, then fired at the ground between them. The shot sliced at her ears, but she cared not for deafness. What was the use of hearing when all she'd hear was laughter and mockery if she failed? She'd return home to a mother who wished her dead and a brother who'd burned her arm. Their voices were nothing, and she didn't need ears to hear the man she loved.

"He doesn't know suffering," she muttered to Aliax. "What does a scion of House Uziokaki know of pain?"

"We all suffer in our own ways," he replied.

"Some, not enough."

Tazper touched her uninjured arm, trying to stop her from raising the gun again. "Kasia, what are you—"

She shoved him away, then aimed at Razamat. "Again!"

"I refuse," Razamat said.

"Then the amber is *mine!* If you believe I've not endured more than lead and blood, Lord Razamat, then you know nothing about me." She pulled back the hammer again. "Another round, or I win."

Razamat stared at his feet for what seemed an eternity before he returned his gaze to her. It resembled one she'd seen from Leonit a thousand times. "Very well."

The silver mercenary repeated her command to ready, but Razamat did not raise his gun. Instead, he just pulled back the hammer and held it to the side.

"Fire!"

Razamat fired into the ground as Kasia screamed and pulled the trigger again and again. Only one shot fired, as she didn't pull back the hammer after the first. But the first was enough.

Crimson burst from the center of Razamat's chest. He stepped back, a hand held over the wound, and his gun slipped from his fingers. His mouth hung ajar as the silvery mercenary ran to him just in time to catch his fall. She shouted for Lazan to save Razamat, that the duel was over, but Lazan looked only to Kasia.

"Wait," Kasia told him before stomping across the twenty strides between her and the Uziokaki scion. Her pain grew with Lazan's magic fading, but she'd done it. Her plan had worked.

Yet she felt no victory.

There had been no challenge in the final round. Razamat had conceded out of spite or pity, and she knew full well that had he chosen to raise his gun a third time, it would've been the last. In the end, though, it didn't matter why he'd conceded. The amber was hers. She would rebuild her house and finally be able to turn her focus to figuring out who had killed her father. An awakened had killed him, but surely, a single spirit couldn't have broken into a great house without aid.

The silver mercenary backed away at Kasia's approach. Blood covered her entire front, and her head was light from blood loss, but Lazan would save her no matter what Razamat said. All that remained to be decided was whether Razamat lived or died.

The scion wheezed on the ground, hands spasming. Kasia stood over him and pulled back her pistol's hammer. When she looked at Razamat, his face morphed into her father's.

It's not him, she told herself, blinking away the illusion. *Father is dead. THEY took everything he built.*

Then she aimed at his head.

"I will order Lazan to save you on one condition," she said as the mercenaries raised their rifles at her threat.

Razamat coughed weakly. "Name it."

She pointed east with her gun still in-hand. "Return to Giamivik and tell Lord Sazilz that my father's border stands. The amber belongs to House Niezik, but House Uziokaki will receive the first season's shipments to sell or keep at your pleasure. The market rates will be high until people realize we've discovered this reserve. Let this be an act of goodwill between our houses for your actions today."

"They won't accept."

"Then try," she snapped, aiming at his head again, "or I shoot you here."

He laid his head back and cackled through the pain. "I'll do it. Just don't let me die with such disgrace."

Kasia holstered her gun before waving for Lazan. Her legs grew weak as he approached, and she knelt, fighting the urge to vomit. Where had that wonderful strength gone? The wounds were only beginning to hurt, but the magic's gradual retreat left her feeling naked. It was as if she'd been shown her true potential, only to have it ripped away minutes later.

"It's fading," she mumbled to Lazan. "Heal me first, then him."

So he did, and she hugged herself as his blood red wisps circled her. They plunged into her skin at each wound. It quickly healed the wounds from the first bullet, which had gone straight through her stomach and out the other side. The other bullet remained lodged in her shoulder, and Lazan's magic pushed it free, forcing her to grit her teeth through the strange pain. When it was over, she touched the wound and found only smooth skin.

The bullet lay in the muck before her. Even coated in blood, the small chunk of lead hardly looked threatening, yet it had nearly killed her. It should've.

She stood when Lazan finished healing Razamat. Her clothes were a disaster, but that was nothing compared to the Body Reacher's paling skin and labored breaths. Realm Taint never left, yet he'd done it for her—and enough money to buy a townhouse in Kalastok. Such decisions only added to the weight on her shoulders. For now, though, her thoughts lingered on the Uziokaki lord.

"Why did you let me win?" she asked Razamat as his mercenaries helped him rise. "You could have killed me with any of those shots, let alone the last."

"There are things greater than serving my prideful patriarch of a cousin." He dusted off his jacket, despite the blood that already coated his front. His expression was more mournful than angry, and he donned his hat once more before replying, "You are a fierce woman, daughter of Leonit. I hope one day that my own daughter may be as bold as the Amber Dame when she must fight for what she believes in."

"The Amber Dame?" she asked, brow raised.

"It is either that or the mad one," he quipped as he waved for his men to bring the horses. "Now, let us be rid of this damned willow. You have given me plenty of riding to do in the coming days, and I have no desire to remain in this shirt for any longer than necessary."

Kasia watched him go, fists clenched at her sides. How could that be it? Razamat had fought her every step of the way, only to fire into the ground when it truly mattered. She couldn't decide whether that was cowardice or bravery greater than her understanding.

A tepid Tazper approached with her horse. His wide-brimmed hat was turned sideways, and he itched his face, not meeting her gaze. "Here is your mount, my lady."

She took the horse, running her hand across its neck as she studied her footman. "You aren't telling me something."

Aliax scoffed in her head. *Can you blame him?*

"You…" Tazper shuffled his feet. "I am worried about you. This amber means a lot, but the woman holding that gun was not the Kasia I know."

"Who was it then?" she asked.

"I don't know for certain, but it frightened all of us. Though you didn't Reach, it was hard not to think about Aliax."

She snatched his arm, squeezing with the latent might of Lazan's magic reinforcing her grip. "Don't you dare mock me with his name! I tried to save him, Taz. I did everything I could…" Tears stung her eyes, so she spun away. Aliax's voice haunted her.

"Did you try to protect me? Or did you try to protect yourself?"

"Shut up!" she snapped, throwing out her arms at the voice, but no one was there.

Sweat streamed down her face when she turned back to Tazper. It was cold, uncomfortable, but her chest burned with her brother's flames, making her wish she could run from herself. But she couldn't run. Her house needed her. More than just her family, thousands of lowborn and minor scions relied on her leadership, and they would starve during the long everdark if she failed to pay them. No, fleeing wasn't an option. This amber was only the first step toward rebuilding House Niezik and avenging her father.

So she stomped to her horse, forcing herself to ignore the voice in her head as she threw herself into the saddle without aid. It was far from smooth, but there would be no use acting around these mercenaries any longer. They had seen the true her in that duel. Tazper had too, and out of the corner of her eye, she saw him staring at her for most of the return ride.

It was a solemn journey despite her success, and upon their return, the Uziokaki mercenaries took their gear and departed with little fanfare. They neither spat at their Niezik rivals nor pressed Razamat for another attempt at the amber. Instead, they kept their distance from Kasia and skirted toward their cart as quickly as they could. Then they were gone with as few words as possible, the drizzle falling on their tall hats and uniformed shoulders until they disappeared over the eastern ridge.

It was over.

Fanzala and Tania waited to hear what had happened, but Kasia left Artaxan to give the report. Her head spun too much after losing Lazan's magic strength. As the scouts started their fires for the night, she shied away, holding her scarred arm. The flames danced behind her eyelids, and she wanted nothing more than to be away from their glow.

A bird's call stopped her strides from her tent. An amber-throated raven—like the ones that had led them to this very grove—fluttered overhead as Kasia raised her hand toward it. She pulled off her glove, and the talon upon her index finger glinted in the dwindling light.

It caught the raven's eye. A chatter rose from its beak as it dove, seeming to drift on the air before landing on her finger and pecking at her talon's crystal. The *tink, tink, tink* reminded her of how Leonit had drummed his taloned hand on his study desk. She'd curl with a book in one of his large chairs and wait for him to play their nightly game of haataamaash. Her heart lightened as she pictured him sitting with his tomes and ledgers, spectacles gripped in one hand and the other running rampant through his gray hair.

But that vision faded to smoke amid her childhood screams. A gunshot echoed through her mind, and she cocked her head, mimicking a target struck by the bullet. The awakened hadn't cared about the shot, though, and the raven on her finger gave no care to her imagination.

"There's no food for you there," she told it, reaching into her shouldered bag with her other hand and pulling out a slice of bread. It showed no interest. "What do you want?"

The raven cocked its head.

Kasia furrowed her brow and pulled out a piece of amber that Artaxan had retrieved during his original scouting mission. No larger than her fingernail, it was golden in the dim duskfall light. "Here. It's far less valuable than crystal, but it matches your throat."

The raven *cawed* in reply before plucking the amber bead from her fingers. It leaped free, its little wings flapping away until it joined its flock among the sea of orange, red, and brown leaves.

Kasia let herself smile as she stared at her talon. It still tickled from the bird's feet, but that sensation distracted from the turmoil in her heart and mind. A reminder of the beautiful things that continued on, regardless of the quarrels between the Commonwealth's scions. Raviak Forest was torn between houses Niezik and Uziokaki, but the creatures dwelling within saw no difference between them. All that mattered to animals was who held a bow and who gave an offering.

It gave her an idea for a new emblem. House Niezik's old one was dated, resembling a minor family's more than the vibrant strength of the great houses. The amber-throated ravens had led them to the amber in a way, and had watched as she'd defeated Razamat. Why not honor them?

Kasia's tent was dark until she lit a small candle in its center. It offered enough light for her to changed out of her bloodied and mud-covered clothes, but no heat. The air stung against her bare skin, like a thousand needles dragged across her body. A faint soreness remained where Razamat had shot her. Phantom pain, she'd heard Body Reachers call it. The wound had healed, but one's mind remembered the impact and needed time to forget.

Some scars lingered longer than others.

Kasia traced the raised sections of the burns along her left forearm. Would she ever forgive Gregorzon for his betrayal? Did he even deserve it?

Her true suffering lurked deeper than burns, soreness, and frigid air, so she let herself sit naked in the cold awhile longer, embracing the pain. It couldn't truly hurt her, not compared to what she sought to bury… and what she needed to fix. She had her amber. It was only the beginning. Somewhere out there was an explanation of her father's death.

She would not rest without revenge.

THE LIST

A day later, Kasia donned Tazper's wide-brimmed hat and strode through the camp's downpour. Her head was heavy enough without the constant drum of water soaking her hair. Tazper had ecstatically relinquished it the moment she asked, but it felt wrong to ask for his help. Had he not done enough for her already?

Her drenched friend led her between two head-high piles of dirt, explaining the progress Fanzala and the scouts had made on the amber mines. Amber was far more fragile than iron or coal. They needed to be careful to ensure the pieces weren't damaged during extraction, so it would've taken far longer without an Earth Reacher to handle much of the labor.

"When will the first shipment be ready?" she asked once he was finished.

He glanced at Artaxan, who shrugged. "It will take time and many more workers, my lady," the chief scout said before holding out an oval-shaped piece. "We have only recovered the first few shards, some containing insects like this one."

Kasia hesitated. Awe and fear both filled her. This was the first of the amber that would bring her the wealth she needed, but so too, did it represent the fragility of her hopes. She'd conned her way to victory this time. House Uziokaki would know, and the great houses did not lose with grace. Leonit had taught her that lesson many times.

She plucked the piece from his fingers. It was larger than her palm, remarkably smooth with the occasional chip or crack spread across it. A black ant lay trapped within. She pitied the creature's struggle against the inevitable. Often, she felt much the same.

"Then I will send all the lowborn labor you need to make it happen," she told Artaxan. "Tazper and I will return to Tystok, as there is little left for us to do here."

Artaxan dug his heel in the mud. "More Earth Reachers would be better. Light ones, too, could help with the everdark coming."

"Each Reacher dragged into these woods costs as much as a hundred lowborn."

"And they're worth every kena."

She glanced in the mine entrance, not tall enough to stand up straight yet. It smelled of muck and lacked the support beams that would be added soon. Lanterns and torches could banish the everdark on the surface, but Artaxan was right. Light Reachers would make work in these tunnels far easier, and the fewer laborers who needed to scamper into the darkness, the better. Unfortunately, Spirit Reachers were far more common than the Reachers she needed.

"I will do what I can to find the Reachers you need," she said, "but I can promise nothing. Anything else?"

Artaxan nodded. "I'll take anything you can give. Tazper has a list of supplies that'll help—especially some more guns in case those Uziokaki show back up."

"Then you'll have them."

It had taken her years to get this far. With the first shipments of amber so close, she wasn't about to lose it to an Uziokaki retaliation now. And they *would* retaliate. The only question was when.

She and Tazper mounted their horses and began the journey back home to Tystok. They were taking a risk by leaving Harizik behind, but greater numbers attracted awakened. The mines would need a Spirit Reacher more than two lone riders. Still, Kasia gripped a glass pendant with each drifter that passed overhead, imagining it diving toward her.

But the days passed without incident or any great conversation. Tazper only gave a silent smile when she returned his hat at the end of the rain, and she didn't press him. Days traveling with a large group had been thoroughly draining, and Tazper would speak when he was ready. The duel had jarred them both. Though she regretted nothing, her outburst frightened her too.

What was happening to her?

This was about more than Aliax's voice. For a moment, she'd lost her grip of what was real. Such slips were unacceptable for a house heir, let alone a matriarch. She didn't know whether she endured Realm Taint or something else, but it couldn't happen again, not when her fate and that of thousands more depended on her decisions.

Kasia breathed a sigh of relief when Raviak Forest gave way to farmland days later. She longed for the comforts of home, and the privacy of her own chambers. So long spent in the company of unwashed men had her wishing not to step beyond her room for a long time.

"What will you do with the amber funds?" Tazper finally asked as their horses' hooves stomped through the muddied ground of Tystok. "We have sold so much in recent years…"

"Our estate needs to be reestablished," she said. "Visitors need to see that House Niezik can no longer be scorned, and that means investing in Tystok too."

Small wooden and brick farmhouses formed the town's outer rim, their barley and wheat fields empty after the harvest. Lowborn work was never done, though. Threshing barns were alight with lanterns as they prepared the grain for the long everdark season. Both barley and wheat would feed Kasia's people and be sold to the rest of the Commonwealth, but just as importantly, that same barley would ensure House Niezik's breweries were active. Alcohol made good profit. The real money was in the gambling halls Leonit had become known for, but even those hadn't provided the income to support House Niezik's dwindling reputation.

"The next time I travel to Kalastok, I will sponsor you as a Reacher," Kasia continued. "I promised to do so years ago, but now, I have the resources to make it happen."

The Buried Temple of the Crystal Mother demanded a hefty tithe for any scions wishing to earn a Reacher talon. Most minor scion family's like Tazper's, House Janka, could hardly afford such a burden. That allowed the great houses to control potential Reachers through sponsorships, but Kasia had no desire to control Tazper. He'd proved his loyalty countless times.

Tazper removed his hat, holding it over his heart. "You... You'd make me a Reacher?"

"I always intended to, but know that I won't be traveling to the capital for some time. My great uncle, Faniz, handles our house's business there."

Kasia exchanged greetings with the lowborn they passed as they found the gravel paths near the town center. Her house's struggle would be over soon. At least in part. Amber extraction took time, and House Uziokaki would profit from the initial shipment. Still, hope lay on the horizon.

"The money will not come immediately either," she said. "Do you trust me enough to wait?"

Tazper bowed his head. "I do, my lady. You have given me more of a chance than I could have hoped for. Though your decisions are often unorthodox, I am honored to be by your side."

"Good, because I intend to discover what caused my father's death. I need people I can trust."

They reached the steel and glass gates at the front of the Niezik Estate. A single guardsman leaned against the stone pillar at the far side, his rifle dangling from his fingers. He looked up from his feet to see their approach.

"Shit!" He scrambled to attention. "Lady Katarzyna... errr... Welcome back, my lady."

Kasia furrowed her brow. "Perhaps I must hire more experienced guards as well. Fools like you will ensure I end up like my father." She waved a dismissive hand. "Open the gate, and when we are gone, it would be best if you kept your focus. There are plenty of men in this town who could hold a rifle and stand still."

The guard thumped his chest, then signaled to another guard inside the grounds, who cranked on the wheel. Kasia pushed her horse to the center of the gates as they creaked open. The moment the gap was wide enough for her to pass through, she trotted onward, sending a kick of gravel over the first guard before meeting the cobblestone path.

Once lined with manicured gardens, the path to the two-story mansion was near overgrown with bushes and drooping trees. Scattered, unraked leaves crunched with each of her horse's strides, and Tazper yelped as a long thorn snagged his coat. He nearly dropped from his saddle before the coat tore.

"To come all this way and rip my favorite coat now," he muttered.

Kasia chuckled. "It appears more gardeners and a tailor are needed as well. Our herdsmen will have given us plenty of wool for trade, and I am sure I can spare a fraction for your *favorite* coat."

He grinned back. "A Reacher talon and a coat, my lady? You threaten to spoil me."

"Then take the horses to their stalls and brush them for me," she quipped, dismounting before the front steps with enough proficiency that she held up her chin. "I cannot have my footman becoming spoiled, can I?"

Tazper dismounted and gave an exaggerated bow. "Your wish is my command." Then he guided the horses down a side path between the trees, heading toward the stables.

The stonework Niezik mansion cast a heavy shadow over Kasia as she climbed the steps, passing between two columns and opening the double doors. No butler awaited her. But Uliusa did.

Her nurse stood alone in the near empty foyer. Stained glass windows lined the walls, casting a rainbow over Uliusa's wrinkled face.

With her hands held behind her back and her neck craning forward more with each year, she appeared a grouchy figure, but Kasia smiled at the sight of her.

"I see Gregorzon has yet to burn our estate to the ground," Kasia said, approaching Uliusa and resting a hand on her arm. "That is thanks to you, I presume?"

Uliusa took her gloved hand in both of hers. "The lad is not as troublesome as you claim, mistress. Our worry was not for him while you were gone, but for you."

"We shared that." Kasia glanced at the lit fireplace in the sitting area, then at the staircase to the bedrooms above. "Did my mother decide to welcome me for once? No? Of course not. Why meet your daughter when you blame her for your husband's death?"

"Dear girl, do not speak like that. Your mother—"

Kasia pulled away, interrupting her, "Is a spiteful bitch. She fled from the world, from us, and left me to lead the house alone! I was twelve, yet she claims all of this is my fault."

She paced away from the fire and freed her hands from the grip of her gloves. They were cracked, red, and exposing them to air left them stinging. Still, she flexed them, eyeing the flames with mistrust. Fire belonged to Gregorzon, not her. It had seared her arm within these very walls, and she cradled her scarred arm against her chest.

Uliusa sighed. "She has tried, but you do not understand how losing one's spouse can break you."

And Uliusa could not understand how losing both father and mother had ruined Kasia. Her mother, Yazia, lived, but she was little more than an infirm ghost who screamed at her daughter's missteps. During the most formative years of Kasia's life, she'd had no mother to guide her into the role of matriarch. Leonit had taught her all he could. A twelve-year-old girl could only understand so much, though, and in the decade since, Uliusa had been Kasia's closest thing to a parent.

"We have the amber," Kasia said absently, staring at the wood floor.

"Your father would have been proud," Uliusa replied.

Footsteps approached from a side door. A boy in his late teens stepped into the room, his wavy hair ashen gray like Kasia's and his frame as narrow as a sapling. He wore thin fabric gloves and an un-buttoned jacket with embroidered crimson designs on the sleeves. When he smirked, his hazel eyes burned in the firelight.

"I highly doubt Father would have admired Katarzyna failing to maintain our prestige," Gregorzon said. "Who did you kill this time, Sister? Another lowborn lover, or an Uziokaki scion?"

Kasia stormed to him, grabbing his shirt and holding her talon to his nose. "No one died for the amber, and I am *dying* to Reach. Do you want to relieve me? Or perhaps you would prefer to descend into the dark mines with only your own fire to light the way?"

"Mother would kill you!"

Uliusa snatched Kasia's arm. "That is enough!"

Kasia pushed her brother away, and Gregorzon stumbled into the wall. "Mother can barely leave her bed," she snapped at her brother. "If you want any of the amber profits, you will help me ensure the mines are efficient. No more sitting here, mocking me with your friends. Either find a place to do real work, or make yourself useful to our enterprises."

Gregorzon frowned, but a question lingered in his eyes. "How did you do it? Those lands are House Uziokaki's by tradition."

Kasia patted the pistol at her hip. "I won a duel." He laughed, but she insisted, "Lord Razamat Uziokaki confronted us with his merce-naries. My attempts to persuade him of our map's legitimacy failed, so I dueled him for three rounds. He shot me twice."

Uliusa gasped, pawing at Kasia's cheek. "Are you well?"

"Body Reacher Lazan Karianam was there to ensure I survived, so worry not. Lord Razamat endured more pain than I did, and he agreed to sway his house in return for the first season's shipments of amber."

"The first *season*?" Gregorzon exclaimed. "That will be the great-est share of profits while prices are high!"

Kasia raised her brow. "Would you have preferred to lose the amber to them entirely?"

"No…"

"Then go tell Mother the good news. My presence would only sour her mood, and I have work to do."

"Should you not bathe first, my lady?" Uliusa asked. "You are quite dirtied from your travels."

Kasia let her have that moment of motherly kindness. "Of course. Draw a bath for me, won't you? I just wish to step into Father's study for a moment."

"*You* are going into Father's study?" Gregorzon replied, arms crossed. "Since when?"

"Times change, Brother." She stepped past him and headed toward the far hall. "The past harrows us all, but I cannot rebuild our house if I cannot sit where he sat. I am unconvinced his death was caused by a rogue awakened alone. We will soon have the funds necessary for me to investigate, so I must see if he left any clues behind."

Not waiting for further appeals, she hurried down the hall. Her heart raced. She'd been too afraid, too *weak*, to return to Leonit's study since that horrific night, and when her fingers graced the door handle, she froze, sweat trickling down her brow. Her father had died just beyond the door. Grief and pain had filled every day since, and Aliax's voice echoed her fears.

"Do you actually deserve to sit where he sat? Leonit built your family into that of a great house. He was King Yaakiin's most powerful minister. What have you done?"

She closed her eyes, cursing under her breath.

"I am not him," she whispered. "But he couldn't save us from his enemies. I need to do more. I need to be more."

Aliax laughed. *"You're a girl out of her depth."*

"When haven't I been?"

Kasia shoved open the door, its creak dulled by the study's decorative rugs and rows of bookshelves. Dust hung in the air along with the smell of leather and parchment. No candles lit the space, but the light from outside revealed Leonit's haataamaash board. Situated on the table between two sofas, its pieces remained where they had that night.

Tears fled Kasia's eyes as she approached the game board and touched her red spy beside the white throne. She'd learned her father's strategy to defeat him, despite his dragon piercing her own defenses.

"Did you let me win?" she asked the ghostly chamber, repeating her question from that night.

"Like that spy slipped through my defenses more easily than a dragon, we cannot always see those who threaten us," her father's reply echoed in her memories.

Had he seen who killed him?

King Yaakiin had died the same night as Leonit, and Kasia had learned well that coincidence was rare in Commonwealth politics. Monstrous awakened never pierced glass-infused buildings, opting for easier kills. That night, it had ignored the servants and guards in the estate. Why would it pursue Leonit deep within the estate if not told to do so?

She toppled her father's throne piece, staring across the board at her own. Who could have done this?

The further half of the study was dark, but she knew it well from countless hours spent with her father. She crossed it to his desk, finding the matches in the top drawer and lighting the gas lamp at the head of it.

The onslaught of light forced her to blink away the dots in her eyes. Once her vision recovered, though, she discovered the tome her father had been reading that night. She held a finger over her nose as she brushed away the dust coating its pages, only to find a book about the history of the Awakening—when the first awakened spirits had emerged from the Spirit Wastes nearly a millennium before, destroying the Piorak Empire and nearly all of civilization.

Her fingers trembled as she read the two visible pages over and over, but they offered no insight. Why had he been researching the Awakening in the first place? He'd served as minister of glass, never studying distant history all that often. At least that she knew of.

She turned her attention to the other desk drawers instead. Leonit's keys had long since been hers, but she'd never sought to open his locked secrets. Even when she'd peeked as a child, he'd scolded her for prying where she didn't belong. Now, though, this was where she belonged. She was sure of it.

The key slid into the first of the two locked drawers with a *clank*. She pulled it open, and a tearful laugh escaped her throat as she retrieved its contents.

The oakwood handle of Leonit's favorite revolver was cold against her palm. She raised it like he had that night, its silver patterns glinting in the lamplight and skulls looking back at her from each chamber. The infamous pistol of Stormrider, an Ogrenian pirate who'd once stalked the northern Vitrian Sea. Leonit may not have discussed ancient history often, but his love of folk tales had been undeniable.

"Bang," she mouthed, imagining Razamat falling back with her bullet piercing his chest.

Guilt came with that memory, so she dropped the pistol on the desk and reached for the last drawer. It slid open with her key, but was empty.

She gave a disappointed huff before something caught her eye. Unlike the smooth willow wood of the rest of the desk, two grooves ran along the side of the inside of the drawer. It was shallower than it appeared to be from the outside too, so she ran her hand across the grooved side and pulled.

Something shifted.

She yanked away her hand away, heart racing. What was this? When she examined the drawer again, the drawer's right side had just barely lifted along the grooves—a false bottom.

What were you hiding in a secret compartment, Father?

Once again, she reached inside and tugged on the raised edge, prying it free to expose a single slip of paper beneath.

Kasia, it said on the visible side. *Find them.*

Kasia's chest tightened as she snatched the paper and slapped it down on the desk, next to the pistol. She could hardly breathe. Was this it? Had her father known she would seek vengeance?

When she couldn't stand it anymore, she flipped the paper over, gripping it so tightly that its edges crinkled.

Raniana Laxis, the peasant spy.

Fantil Tozki, the traitorous sergeant.

Parqiz Uziokaki, the Spirit Reacher. He knows the names of the rest.

Find the Crimson Court. Find those who killed me.

The note slipped from Kasia's fingers as she fell back into her father's chair. This list… It had been here the whole time, waiting for her to open the desk. How had she been such a coward? All these years she'd hoped for answers.

Instead, she had names. And soon, she'd have the funds to challenge the great houses.

She drummed her taloned finger against the desk as Leonit had so many times, staring down at the note. Three names. Three targets who'd helped assassinate her father. Whoever this Crimson Court was, she would find them. She'd sought Death's power to exact her revenge.

Now she would have it.

Razamat had called her the Amber Dame—mad, but fierce. So be it. These Crimsons had taken everything from her, and Crystal be damned, she would make them suffer a thousand times for each day she'd endured without her father.

Kasia snatched Leonit's revolver and stood where he had in his final moments. The air was cold with the study's fireplace long since extinguished, but her throat burned as she aimed the gun at the open door. Her arm had wavered against Razamat. Now, as she pulled back the hammer, she held firm. She finally had her foe, her chance at revenge. And she would not fail.

Click.

The hammer fell when she pulled the trigger, but no shot followed. She frowned, checking the cylinder. Five chambers were full. The last lay empty, and her heart sank knowing it had been Leonit's final shot. A bullet for a spirit—useless.

She threw the gun beside the haataamaash board and fell back onto the sofa as exhaustion took over. Just days before, she'd had neither targets nor the money to take her vengeance. She'd been nothing more than an upstart matriarch of a fallen house. Oh, how such little time could change everything.

Taking her red spy from the board, she held it into the light emanating from the lamp. It seemed to bleed as her fingers left streaks across a decade of dust.

"I'll find you," she whispered to the Crimsons who'd slain her father. "And when I'm finished, there will be nothing left of you— body or spirit."

Then she tucked the piece into her pocket and headed for the door. She had her amber, but her work was far from finished. The Crimson Court would not rest.

Neither would the Amber Dame.

END OF THE AMBER DAME

A Word from the Author

These novellas can be a fun break from writing expansive main books, and *The Amber Dame* is no exception. I had always planned on telling the story of Kasia acquiring her nickname and rising in prominence. More importantly, though, I wanted to show the beginnings of her progressing Realm Taint

Alternatively, prequels are difficult, because there are some reading this who have read *The Crimson Court* and those who have not. I wanted to lightly introduce some concepts that get more thoroughly fleshed out in the main books along with ensuring those of you looking for Kasia' backstory have the chance to experience something new with her character and the world. I definitely enjoyed writing a more inexperienced Kasia, still pushing toward to recover her fallen house. Hopefully you did too!

If you have enjoyed reading this story, please take the time to post an honest review on whatever retailer you purchased this book from (or on Goodreads or social media sites). Every review helps new readers discover my books, and personal recommendations are more powerful than anything I can say as an author.

-      Brendan

ABOUT THE AUTHOR

Brendan Noble is an American author writing epic fantasy with inspiration from his Polish ancestry, mythology, video games of all types, and Dungeons & Dragons. He loves to explore the complexities of politics and the gray between good and evil.

Shortly after beginning his writing career in 2019, Brendan married his wife Andrea and moved to Rockford, Illinois from his hometown in Michigan. Since then, he has published three series: The Realm Reachers, The Frostmarked Chronicles, and The Prism Files.

Outside of writing, Brendan is a data analyst and soccer referee. His top interests include German, Polish, and American soccer/football, Formula 1, analyzing political elections across the world, playing extremely nerdy strategy video games, exploring with his wife, and reading.